MW01113737

LEFT THE GHETTO

LEFT THE GHETTO

Sherri Lynn Kelley

iUniverse, Inc.
New York Lincoln Shanghai

LEFT THE GHETTO

All Rights Reserved © 2004 by Sherri Lynn Kelley

No part of this book may be reproduced or transmitted in any form or by any means, graphic, electronic, or mechanical, including photocopying, recording, taping, or by any information storage retrieval system, without the written permission of the publisher.

iUniverse, Inc.

For information address:
iUniverse, Inc.
2021 Pine Lake Road, Suite 100
Lincoln, NE 68512
www.iuniverse.com

ISBN: 0-595-31795-2

Printed in the United States of America

This book is dedicated to:

My Mother

The Late
Joyce Ann Kelley
10–4–1946 9–23–1999

Contents

INTRODUCTION

In the ghetto and on the streets about a single mother with four children and she is an alcoholic and do drugs everyday. Her kids' fathers are nowhere around only to see the children when its possible. The environment that Pebbles and her kids live in is not suitable for kids. Pebbles have three girlfriends and their names are Yonnie, Martha and Danielle and they hang out everyday. Tia, Pebbles daughter who is the oldest of her sisters is the one that is going to work hard and get out of the ghetto. And don't ever come back not even to visit her mother and sisters who stays there. Tia seems to forget about how she was raised up and the struggling taking care of her sisters and her mother. Growing up in the house with consent people there everyday and no food most of the time. Tia seems to stay in school and graduates. Pebbles the mother tries her hardest to stay away from drugs but the people and the environment was very impossible. She had try to change with every man she meets but it seems something don't work out right. And she ends up doing the same thing over and over again. Her girlfriends try to give advice but the advice they give is negative. Because they don't want her to get nowhere in life. Pebbles parents try helping her time after time. And over and over again she lets them down. Her sister Donna tries talking to her but, Pebbles does not listen. Because the truths hurts when you are an addicted and people doesn't see things your way. Pebbles just make things seem so difficult why she cannot do the right thing. Pebbles is one tough black women who don't bite her tongue for no-one. And ready for anything that comes her way. Her man Big-Cal had fed her all the drugs and got her hooked. And left her in the ghetto to face the world in her boxing gloves.

CHAPTER 1

TIA

Well I am only 9 years old and my mother seems to not get Shayla and me up for school. But I had got up just in time to get ready and got my sister up also. Going to my mothers' bedroom, I had notice she had company from the night before. And it wasn't her boyfriend Robbie it was who knows. But I seems to get ready, I looked in the refrigerated and it's really nothing there. But if I hurried up me and my sister could eat breakfast at school. Well Shayla didn't have any clean clothes so, I let her wear something of mine. My sister is a size smaller than me. Shayla she is seven years old and she is very cute. My mom says that she looks like her father Big-Cal. I try to do her hair alot when my mother is partying with her friends. She will do our hair and try to cook, until her boyfriend Robbie comes. And then she is stuck in the bedroom or she be with her loud girlfriends when they come around. My mother is a very pretty women not fat at all. She always pulls her hair back to keep it out of the way. Well she is having another baby and it should be here soon. And that's all I hear my mother talk about. Is having the baby and how, Robbie will be in the house with it. She says she don't have the time at all. My father name is Bruce and he comes and picks me up. And does things with me, him and his girlfriend. They read books to me and I think that's why I could read so well. I will be ten years old in another month my father says that he is coming to pick me up. And take me to the fun center with my cousins. My father lives in the surburban area with his girlfriend and her daughter who is two years old. His girlfriend really doesn't come to the house with my father when he picks me up. Because my mother told my father if he brings the tramp here what she was going to do. So that's something my father don't do. Shayla father don't come get her at all. He is in jail for something he did wrong. My mother doesn't talk about him to her. But my sister knows who her father is and his name. Well I finally made it to school and my teacher is giving a quiz today. I'm hoping I passed it that's all I do is read and waits for school to begin. My mother tells me, I am to much like my father. Well I am home from school and it seems like the whole neighborhood is sitting in the living room. I opens up the door and, Ms. Yonnie my mother's girlfriend falls at my foot. She scared me and I said Ms. Yonnie are you alright and she says. Child your, Anut Yonnie had click one too many beers today. She gets up and stumble out of the door hollering. See ya later Pebbles girl. I said hi mom and sat next to her rubbing her stomach. My mother is smiling telling her friends my baby Tia always rubs my stomach. I know this baby is going to be smart just like her. Because she is always giving it her touch. Well Tia your mother is cooking today. I know it looks like, I have been sitting here drinking all day. But really I only had two drinks, I am cutting down until the baby comes. I had promised Robbie that. Well I wondered where the hell is he at didn't see him in two days. And he don't want Pebbles come looking for him. And its not going to be a pretty scene he thinks he's playing somebody. Pebbles is telling her neighbor Martha and she is falling asleep.

Martha doesn't have any kids at all she lives with an old man. Old enough to be her father. Well, Martha girl I know I better start dinner. I had pick up some groceries early today when everybody was sitting around talking. Well I know I need to get started. Pebbles wobbles out to the kitchen and started dinner and everybody had ease out the door. So there is no one home but my mom and me and Shayla. Here comes my sister and she sitting in the kitchen watching my mother prepared dinner. Well I am so happy it is a little quiet now. And I have my mother all to myself for a change me and Shayla. Well it is time for bed and we get to watch some television. Since my mom boyfriend Robbie is not there. We only have one television in the house and my mom wants it in her bedroom. We did have a telephone but it had got disconnected. And no cable television just regular stations that comes in. Well its night time and I guess no one will be knocking on the door. Because sometimes that happens all night long. But everybody just left so I guess they are also in for the night.

CHAPTER 2

PEBBLES

Well I am just on my third child and the nurse's comes and make visits. Making sure I am not drinking and drugging with this baby. Because when I was pregnant with Shayla she was a crack baby. Not that I wanted it that way so much pressure and the people around and lets say the environment. My momma keeps telling me to come back home. Yell, right like I am a child all over again. I am with my babys daddy at this moment. His name is Robbie and he run around alot with other women. And I just put up with it. Because I don't want everybody keep talking about me. Saying just having babies and daddies leave. Well I am going to hang in there with this man. Tia is my oldest baby she will be ten years old. And she is just as smart as she can be. Well, I thinks she picks that up from her daddy. Bruce Mayer that's his name well he had left me. When Tia was just three months old and he said that he'll take care of the baby. But he doesn't want anything to do with me. Just threw me out like, I was trash or something. And that's when I started drinking and smoking crack trying to ease the pain being alone with a baby. But things got worse because I had another baby. And that was Shayla and she was a crack baby. Child Protective Service is on my back. And my momma and daddy and family is all on my back. That's why I try so hard not to drink. But if everybody was in my shoes they will know it's not easy. It's so easy to get hooked on drugs but it is so hard to get off of it. Robbie says he's going to stay with me. But how can I know he's telling the truth when he's messing around on me. My girlfriends I only have three of them. They do the same thing I do. Don't work drink and be bugging and drugging like I do. Well my baby is due very soon now. And I know I have to straighten up my act. And stop hanging around people who is not positive. I know my momma think that's what I am going to do all my life, but I am not. One day I am going to get it right. When I was a little girl. I always wanted to lived like on an island some where like the rich people. But when you are a little girl you always think thats going to happen when you get older. When I got pregnant with Tia, I was very scared to tell my momma and daddy. I thought that they were going to put me out on the streets. Because I was nineteen years old still living at home. And living at home is cheaper than getting your own place. And my momma and daddy didn't have a baby around them so long. Because all their kids are grown. But no my momma didn't have a fit or anything. She was so calm and quiet asking me questions. Like how was I feeling and is I'm alright. My daddy was the one who was having a fit. Hollering where is that Bruce at and Is he still with you knowing a baby is on the way. My daddy loves all his daughters no matter what we done or he heard we have done. My daddy was cool as ice. And when Tia was born you should have seen the big grin on my daddy's face. Oh yes! he was a proud grandfather for real. He had his camera that he hasn't used in so long. He had to wipe the dust off it. Well the feeling of being a mother made me want to do the right thing. Yes! my baby Tia was pretty as a button. I didn't really have to buy anything for her.

The family brought alot of her things. I had to go on public aid and food stamps to support my baby. And I think that's where all my problems started. Free money didn't have to work hard at all. And all my girlfriends were on it. Seeing each other at the welfare bank laughing and giggling at one another. Talking about our men and our babies daddy's. Yell it was cute at the time. Baby's daddy's don't stay at all they move on and leave you behind. Men they always have a reason to leave. When you try so hard and that's when the drinking and drugging starts. Because we are so young and weak at the time. We don't stop to think we jump to the fastest solution there is. Being on public aid is a bitch sometimes. They asked 100 questions to keep your money coming. What is the father name? Shit how about I didn't know who the father is. And give them the name of a wine-o who sleeps on a stoop. They come looking for him and he's sixty years old can't make babys. And probably stay to drunk to remember that he can't. Well Bruce he thought he was above me and used Tia to get his women. Yell he thought he was coming to my momma and daddy's house with a bitch to pick up my baby. Hell No! Because Pebbles was not having it not that day or no other day. Even thou I wasn't working. I was the bitch holding the cards. Bruce always had something to complain about. And 99% of the time I wasn't in the mood to hear it. It wasn't easy carrying the baby for nine months and it wasn't easy giving birth. And it surely aint easy living with your mom and dad. My mom would watch every move I had made with the baby. Shoot! A grown women at home but your mom treating you likes you a child. My dad he was just cool as ice. And when my mom and me was each other necks my dad was there like a referee breaking it up. And my mom was hollering at my daddy saying when do Sandra Cook do wrong huh! And only time she says my birth name is when she is burning up hot. And me I love it because I can see somebody is on my side. Knowing damn well I was wrong. And the rest of the day my mom stays out of Pebbles way. Well I needed my own place for real but thinking about it. There wouldn't be no more live in babysitter for Pebbles. But I had to do something I had just turn twenty years old and I am still at home. All my girlfriends have the public housing and it has a waiting list. That's what I had went on and did. Having my own place was so wonderful. I didn't get a phone for a while. Because I didn't want my parents calling seeing who would pick up the phone. And really I was just being a bitch. Pebbles was holding the cards with her rules. Finally! Shoot I should have got my own place a long time ago. I was just being cheap and putting up with somebody else rules. It was nice living by myself. Tia was fifteen months old now with her own room. I had met many of men and many of men seem all the same full of shit if you asked me. Knowing they got another women and sit there like you is the only one. Well I did like one man in particular and he was Calvin Tucker. Yes! Amen he really knew how to treat a lady well he address all his women as ladies. He was my everyday supplier and all I did for him was easy as a pie. Well I end up getting pregnant with Shayla. And here comes more crap my mom have to talk about. To her nosy friends she talks to on the phone everyday. And they say they are christians. You would think they talked about the bible or something. When I was a kid my mom use to burn up the food on the stove gossiping. Talking about everybody and everything. Well Calvin everybody calls him Big-Cal. I was crazy in loved with him or was it the drugs he was feeding me. Well put it this way whatever it was I was feeling good about him and the fact. I was carrying his baby in my belly. Before I had given birth to Shayla. Big-Cal had gotten arrested for a huge amount of crack cocaine. And the judge had sentenced him to five years in jail. Well I had cried for days and days. I am pregnant again no baby daddy around. And I really let the people and my family get to me. So I had escape pumping myself with the drugs and alcohol. Not even caring if I die. Taking care of Tia by myself and another baby on the way. Now what Pebbles going to do.

CHAPTER 3

PEBBLES

Shayla was born and was a crack baby and was I in trouble. I had to call my mom on the phone and ask her to come to the hospital. I had told her that I think they going to take the baby. She is hollering Pebbles take the baby. For what huh! And I didn't have any choice at the time. I'm crying mom please come to the hospital. So my mom didn't ask any more questions and she came but my dad didn't. I can hear my mother and the child protective service talking in the hallway. And I can hear my mom tell the lady that she didn't have any ideal. That her daughter was on drugs and on it heavy. And my mom was asking her now what is going to happen. Well the lady was telling my mom they do have choices. That the baby can go in foster care. Or someone in the family can take the baby. And then she told my mom that the baby can come home. But I would have to go in a program and a visiting nurse stops in at my house. It seems like the whole world was coming down on me all at once. My man is in jail and my baby is a crack baby. Lying in the hospital just thinking. Damn! How could I do this to myself and my dad wont even come to the hospital. I am wondering what is he thinking of is he mad at me. Well I had went into the program and the purpose of doing it. To get child protective services off my back. And get through the program and get back to bugging and drugging. Tia loves to have the baby around. Sometimes I thought she was the mom. She wouldn't let no one get close to Shayla it was like a bond my babies had. Well child protective services is still stopping at the house. She be talking and I don't hear her at all. I just want her to get her white ass out of my house. I guess they think I don't love my babies. My home girls, Martha and Yonnie they don't have kids. My baby sitters when I want to get away to a motel. And get blazed with one of the dealers. And my other home girl Danielle she has one kid. And the father is taking care of it. Danielle doesn't talk much about her business and Pebbles do respect that. Because what I do when I'm away from my girlfriends is my business. Just that and very simple. And I very much make that clear. A girlfriend sometimes is best not to have at all. It seems like they just there to know your business and as soon as they get mad. You better believe it. They are telling everything they know. Well having babies around and full responsiblity everyday. Tia getting into everything and Shayla is starting to walk. It seems like all the men I was sleeping with just came at night and left in the morning. It seems so drastic but you cannot make a man do anything he doesn't want to do. And I felt like this, I'm not looking for a father for my babies at all. They have a father even if they are not there. And it's not anyone business why they didn't stick around. And yes Pebbles gets an attitude when people question her about it. It seems like black women is always in another women business. But when something happens to them, they got their mouth shut and seal. When I was in the program. I had an attitude on wheels. You got to get up and talk and that was something. I didn't want to do at all and at that time. I realized that I had a problem. A problem that grew big through the years. I kept in touch with Big-Cal on and off. I had blamed him for all my troubles. And why shouldn't I? It was so much pressure at times. And getting another man to make me feel special was hard. Why us black women need a man to get us by. But my heart was with Big-Cal. My babies Tia and Shayla were my comfort zones. But to tell the social workers and my family. They would swear that I'm just saying that. No one knows how I feel and I guess no will find out. Christmas comes and it's hard to buy for two children. And the men I was sleeping with didn't care if my children had toys or clothes. Didn't want to ask my sister Donna for any money. She buys gifts for the girls and my family also does to. My mom and family just sit back and watch to see what Tia and Shayla gets for Christmas. And all my money mostly goes to my habit. Well I had bumped into my girlfriend from high school. And she was telling me to call my social worker that handles my public case. And my worker had sign me up for the adopted family. Who helps single mothers on Christmas. Well I did that and they had brought alot of gifts for Tia and Shayla. And even some for me. My girls was happy and I was happy. And you should have seen the eyes on my family. Yes shock! Well I got through that and it was easy to fool my family. I had learned alot of tricks and schemes. To get what I wanted through the years. My sister Donna never really come and visits me. She thought she was better than everybody. Always telling me bitch get your shit together. Giving the Cook's a bad name look at you. I would put her ass out of my house. Shit she come univited when she do come. I don't go knocking on her door without her inviting and thinking about it. She doesn't invite me to her apartment. She be thinking somebody going to steal something because they do drugs. And my life things got worse and my babies were getting older. And Tia always had watch over Shayla. It was alot of people in my house all the time. Fights would break out in the house all the time. Where it was always someone stealing someone else's rocks. Tia alot of time was with her father and Shayla would be with my mom. My mom said she would take Shayla over there with her. She said she doesn't need to be around my friends. I was so happy for that but alot of times. I wish my mom were hard on me. But she said that if she told me don't do it. I was going to do it anyway. Well my life in general was my drugs and my men. Big-Cal had got out of jail finding out he didn't love me at all. He had somebody else another bitch. And check this out a son who happens to be the same age Shayla is. Damn! Well life goes on like they say. Shayla had seen him a couple of times. I was so hurt and I had waited all those years for him. He had my heart and only him. But thats what men do they bring you down and they move on. I was considered as Pebbles the crack head. I try so hard to get off of the shit. And this one time I had made up in my mind to get off of it. I would stop everybody for coming in my house. And sometimes when they knock. I wouldn't open the door at all. Tia is in the second grade and Shayla had just started kindergarten. And I had tried to change my ways and be a good mother. I was always at the school being a parent helper in Shayla class. My girlfriends was sitting back talking about me. Yell because they didn't want to see me do well for myself at all.

CHAPTER 4

BACK TO DRAMA

Well I had started looking good feeling good about myself. My mom and dad were happy for me. But one thing my neighborhood was bad. People all over the place. And when I go outside my door it was fear in my heart. And I wanted to stay clean for me. I wanted to do something for myself this time. The hell with the people my back stabbing girlfriends and everything. I had my babies and they loved me. Tia was doing well in school and my Shayla also was doing well. But everytime I go out in the neighborhood everybody wants to give me drugs. Put it all in my face and they seen that I wanted to do the right thing. Well I had ran into one of my lover's I was dealing with in the past. At the food market and I haven't been with a man in while. So I had invited him over his name was Robert but everyone calls him Robbie. And damn did I fuck up! He brought his pipe and drugs. When I took my first hit it seems like I just got high yesterday. I was picking up where I left off at. Everything started to happen all over again. But this time I had Robbie and I had let him move in. I didn't want to be alone this time around. And the fact that Big-Cal didn't want me at all. But I didn't put up with Robbie bullshit at all. he was getting on my nerves and cheating. But Pebbles had to show a player something. I would leave and let Bruce take Tia over his house. And I let my mom keep Shayla. And I have his cheating ass sitting in the house waiting for me and the kids to come home. He is not going to play me and living in my damn house. I come home two days later with a smile on my face. No care in my heart telling Robbie now how do it feels the shoe on the other foot. He just sits there and calls me all kinds of crack heads and whores. It didn't matter what he called me. I had told him the next time you stay out all night. And you in my house take your shit with you. OK PLAYER! Robbie gives me that look like damn. Pebbles had walked over the other side of the room. Picking up her over night bag and walking up the stairs. And then she turns around and says to Robbie now call your mother and tell her that. You tell her everything else. Well Robbie turns out to be a momma's boy. And I know his mom don't like me but who cares. Shit! She can take her damn big baby over there with her. Well let me get ready and go and visit one of my girls. I try not to have all the people in my house hanging out. My babies had seen the good side of me when I was clean. Well as Pebbles were getting herself together to get ready to leave. And you know that Robbie is sitting down stairs. Waiting for her to leave so he can call his mom. Pebbles is out the door and now Robbie is peeping out the window. To see if she is not standing in the front of the house. Robbie says to his self she's going finally. Now I can call my mom. Robbie is moving stuff out of the way looking for the phone. He finds the phone dialing his mother phone number it rings three times. His mom answers the phone in a very gentle voice saying hello. Mom its Robbie, Pebbles and me had got into another issue over here. His mother is just listening as she always does. Robbie is telling his mom well Pebbles stayed out for two nights straight in a row. And she comes back like she didn't do anything. She is driving me crazy. Well his mother in her low voice telling Robbie to calm down. Robbie sounds like he wants to cry telling his mom. And Pebbles does what she want. And she is with other men in my face. And she says that I'm cheating his mother asked him well baby is you cheating. Because if you are. You are asking for trouble staying in her house. Well mom, Robbie saying I have friends but nothing serious. And Robbie goes saying Pebbles is being with other men for drugs and money. And she is always telling me that I can get out of her house. If I didn't like what she's doing. Robbie mother cuts him off and saying well baby you know you can come back home. Because you do have somewhere to go and you let her know that. Pebbles is not at home yet and theres a knock on the door. It is Tia and her father Bruce. Robbie opens the door and Tia and her father enters the house. Bruce is looking around as he always does and he says hey man what's up. Bruce looks at Tia asking her is she going to be alright until her mother comes home. Tia says yes daddy, I have some home-work to do. Tia gave her dad a peck on the cheek and her father leaves. Bruce is leaving going to his car. Hoping he doesn't bump into Pebbles because thats another argument. In the house Robbie is tell-ing Tia that he is going to cook dinner for everybody. Tia just stand there and listens hoping her mother comes home soon. Robbie is in the kitchen and all you can hear is pots and pans. Tia had finished her homework and it had started to smelling good in the house. Shayla had came in the house her grandmother had drop her off. And drove off when she walks in the house. Shayla says hi Robbie is my mommy home huh! Robbie is now wiping his hands with a towel saying no baby girl she's not home yet. Robbie tries to show the side of him the good person. Someone the girls can look up to when their momma is out doing lord knows what. At this time Pebbles is at her girlfriend Martha's house hanging out. Talking loud and just having herself a good time. Pebbles telling everybody the last time I had good time. Was when I was home with my mom and lets not forget dad. Hey everybody Robbie is my man he's a good man wouldn't trade him for another one. Martha is drunk telling Pebbles to shut up. And she says he's cheating on you. And I seen him with that young girl with both eyes. Pebbles telling Martha shut up you fat cow. Pebbles is still going on and she is saying you can't even get a man your age. You have to go down to the senior citizen bingo night and grab one of those old men. Martha is looking at Pebbles saying well you know that is not funny at all. Pebbles are laughing and everybody who is sitting in the room is laughing. Well at this time Robbie and the kids are home waiting for Pebbles to get in. And finally at three am here comes Pebbles and she is in a very good mood. And he is not saying much to keep it that way. Well Pebbles is in the bathroom running her bath water. She walks back in the room and says to Robbie. I'm going to show you something and you will have a big smile on your face all week long. Robbie is now woke and feeling good. And oh! Pebbles were showing him all morning that she is his women. And after the fact. Robbie was smiling all week cleaning the house taking care or Tia and Shayla. And he was even nice enough. To tell Pebbles to go on out and enjoy herself with her girlfriends. Two weeks later Pebbles is over her moms and dads visiting. Her mom was so surprised to see her and without the girls. Her mom is hurrying up off the phone a place where you can find her. Pebbles shyly saying hi mommy. Pebbles dad is watching t.v. and acting like he is really into it. He doesn't want to be put in the middle of anything. That goes on between a mother and daughter. Pebbles is sitting down not knowing what her mom is going to say next. Alot of times visits at my moms is not nice at all. Well here goes this womens mouth. Well Pebbles you know I've been hearing gossip about you. And baby girl it's not good things. I heard a man is living with you is that true. At this Pebbles is giving her mom a look that could kill. Yes! Mom it's true and what else did you hear. Shit! I'm tired of everytime I come here you telling me something you heard. Mom if I didn't tell you the things you heard. That means I didn't want you to know. Ok at this time Pebbles mother is sweating and heated up. She is hollering ok you bring your ass in my house. And disrespect me and think it's alright. I am your mother and when you are in my house. You're not going to talk to me in that tone of voice young lady. And oh another thing. I heard Big-Cal had got married to his son's mother. Yes married; And at this time Pebbles wants to get out of there and go anywhere. My mom knows what to say to hurt me but this time she can pronounce me DEAD.

CHAPTER 5

PEBBLES DISAPPEARS

It is a week later and Robbie cannot find Pebbles. She has not came home and no one has not seen her. Robbie had never met Pebbles parents. But he knows he has to get in touch with her family he has her kids and taking care of them. Robbie is on the phone talking to his mother. And the only thing she's telling him that she will come home sooner or later. Robbie looks in the phone book and he looks up Mr. and Mrs. Daniel Cook. He started dialing the number and hoping that her parents are nice people. The phone rings three times, Pebbles mom answers the phone. Robbie is nervous and he started out saying hello is this Mrs. Cook. Sandra Cook mother Pebbles mom who is on the other side of the phone says; yes this is her who is calling. Well this is Robert Duncan but everybody calls me Robbie. Pebbles mom sounds very anxious well Robbie what is it you want. Robbie started off saying Mrs. Cook, I cannot find Pebbles. She haven't came home in a week no one has not seen her. Pebbles mom is just sitting there holding the other end of the phone. Not knowing what to say next getting herself together. Asking Robbie have you called the police departments or the hospitals. Well if you didn't check those places don't you think you should? Robbie was not expecting the drama he is just looking for Pebbles. And the sounds of Mrs. Cook have not seen her daughter. So Robbie had decided to end the phone call. He don't want to end up in an argument especially with someone he doesn't know. Well Mrs. Cook I will keep in touch with you have a good day. And Robbie hangs up the phone quickly. Now at this time Pebbles mom is just holding the phone in her hand. And can't believe what just had happen. Turning to her husband Daniel getting his attention away from the television. He is always sitting in his chair all day with the remote in his hand. She is hollering Daniel, he is sitting in his chair flicking channels. Thelma says well listen your daughter Pebbles is missing and I'm going out to find her. He turns and say that gal is going to get you into alot of shit. Thelma turns to him and says what the hell does that mean. You just sit there on your old retirement ass in that chair all day and flick, click that damn remote. While your doing that see if you can find one of those buttons to make you disappear. And another thing you're the reason why she's like that. I'm going to say what I have to say and then. I'm taking your car to look for her. Pebbles mom been wanting to tell her husband for years what's she about to say. Daniel listen up the girl is using drugs all the time because you had let her down. When she had Shayla in the hospital you didn't even come out there to see her or the baby. And when she gets in trouble you sit there and act like you don't care at all. Damn what is your problem oh, I'm going to tell you your problem is you cannot accept the fact your baby girl is a crack head. Wake up and face reality and now she is missing. But, I'm not going to sit here and beg you to help me find her. So, I'm taking your car out there in the hard streets of the ghetto. And I'm going to find my baby girl. Thelma is going out the door thinking what to do next. She is saying to herself damn I'm getting to old for this shit. That girl knows better well I need to stop by Donna's job. And let her know what's going on with her sister. Shit, Donna will help me look for her sister. And I know she will go over to her house and check on it. Damn, I forgot that so called boyfriend is there with the girls. Well I need to get over there. But after I call the police departments and check the hospitals. She has got to be some where. Thelma is driving Daniel's pretty cadillac through the rough neighborhoods kids out playing. People sitting on the stoops watching the big car drive by. Thelma doesn't see anyone that looks familiar. Well not thinking the worse. I know I shouldn't have told her about Big-Cal. Is, I'm the reason why she can't be found. Thelma is just driving and talking to herself. God I only want the best for her. I didn't mistreat her raising her up. I try to show my daughters how a young lady should act. Oh God please let my baby be alright. God you know I care about my girls. And as Thelma is praying she drives up. On some of Pebbles girlfriends that knows her. Thelma hollers out the window saying hey girls. The two females looks to see whom the lady was in the nice looking car. And one of them says hi Mrs. Cook are you looking for Pebbles. Everybody is looking for her she had left the kids with her boyfriend. So Thelma is not saying much. She learned that the less you say the more you will find out what's going on. So Thelma goes on saying well girls you keep looking for her and listening out you know where I lived at. You can come there if you hear anything ok. So the two females said ok Mrs. Cook. Thelma is driving off saying to herself. Where is the hell is that girl at. It seems that no one has seen her. Well I'm headed over to Donna's job to see if she can calm my nerves. Donna works at a doctor's office as a secretary. The doctor's office really don't be busy all the time which is good. I can stop by and talk with her and it's almost time for her to get off of work soon. Because lord knows I needs her support. Donna will find her sister and will get into her ass. About the stupid bull shit she's out there doing. She thinks that life is a game and she needs to get that Big-Cal out of her system and heart. That man doesn't want her he got what he wanted. Shit! He was feeding her drugs so I guess she thinks thats love. Yell that make me feel good about myself drug. Well these young girls today don't know love if it was looking them in their face. Because you lay with a man that don't mean the man is going to be there in the morning. And these days a man makes you pregnant. Your only his baby momma and thats all. Telling Pebbles that is wrong because it's the truth. And like they say the truth hurts. Well here I am at Donna's job and I'm looking beat down and tired right about now. Donna is on the phone making an appointment with a patient. She looks up with a surprise look on her face. Thelma is sitting down looking at Donna waiting to get her attention. Donna's phone call has ended and she hangs up the phone. And she says hi mom is it something wrong at the house. So Thelma says baby nothing is wrong at home. But your sister she has left the kids with her new boyfriend and had been missing for over a week and no one has seen her. That's my death and tears are just flowing down her face. Donna is just standing there wanting to cry seeing her mother in that state of mind. Donna is talking softly saying come on and get it together. Pebbles are somewhere and she will come home. Thelma is lifting her head up and just said in a sobbing voice. Did I raise you girls up right?

CHAPTER 6

ROBBIE

Robbie is now at home taking care of Tia and Shayla. Explaining to them over and over again. That their mommy is alright and she will come home soon. Shayla just keeps crying and she will not eat much. And it seems that everyone been here looking for Pebbles. Martha comes over the house knowing damn well Pebbles is not here. Robbie opens the door she freely walks in. And Robbie start saying Martha what the hell do you want. Did I invite you in here Martha is drunk and high as a kite. At this time Martha is trying to stand up straight. And saying what she have to say without falling down. Martha started off saying Robbie what's up the word out there Is Pebbles just got you here only to baby sit her kids. Robbie walks inside from the front door. He puts his hand on Martha shoulder and says look it's time to leave. And you need to mind your business. Martha is now hollering business your business is all out there in the streets. And I told Pebbles I seen you cheating. The undercover brother you are just like the rest of us around here fool. And now I'm leaving on my own. Robbie says don't fall walking out the door. At this time Martha is going wobbling down the street with her big ass. Well it wasn't long that

Tia's father Bruce found out that Pebbles was missing. He had been here and was mad as hell. He had took Tia with him and just told me to tell Pebbles to call him. So now it's just me and Shayla. And Shayla is starting to feel lonely because her sister is going. I really feel for Shayla no father around. And her mother just leave without even trying to check on her kids. Damn Martha probably is telling the truth I'm just here to baby sit. It seems that one thing after another starts to happen. Robbie had clean the house and got Shayla together for bed. And he had sat down on the couch to look at some television. Down stairs in the living room and I had dose off to sleep. It is in the middle of the night and there is a loud knock on the door. Robbie had jump in his sleep. He got up half asleep to answer the door. He opens the door on the chain where there is just a crack. Something he started doing after the visit from Martha. He thought it was the police with bad news or something. It was a young boy looking like the age 17 or 18 years of age. He had never gave Robbie the chance to say anything. The young boy went off saying Yo! are you Pebbles man. And Robbie said yell whats up have you seen her. The young boy said Yo! dude I seen her and she stole my pack. When she was in my ride. Robbie is now taking a deep breath he don't know what he came there to do. Robbie starts talking real fast saying look Pebbles haven't been here in like over a week now. The young boy just went on saying tell your women. That I would have gave it to her she didn't have to take it. Yo! tell her she owe me that favor and she knows what it is. And he walks off to his brand new ride sitting out there and drives off. Robbie is kind of relieved and he goes back and lays down on the couch. Now its morning and Shayla is up. Robbie is getting her ready for school and he is fed up with everything at this point. He is taking care of kids thats not his. Sitting back waiting for her to come home. He gets Shayla off to school he is just sitting there thinking real hard. Robbie knows that she can't be dead and that she's not in jail. And she have been seen and yell by one of those damn dealers. Suddenly he grabs the phone book flipping through the pages. As he's trying to figure out what number to call. But the phone begin to ring and Robbie couldn't believe it at all. It was a lady from the bendigo rehab for women wanting to talk to a Robert Duncan. With a smile on his face like God has answer his prayers. The voice on the other side of the phone goes on saying. Is this Robert Duncan I'm speaking with. Robbie goes on saying yes, yes this is him. Mrs Truman from the bendigo rehab says she's fine and she's getting rest at this time. Well I'm making this phone call to give you some information on how our program is run. The lady continues Sandra Cook had check in here at five a.m. in the morning. She gets one phone call a day this is a thirty day program there is no visiting days at all. The method of this program to give them the help they come in here seeking. At this time Robbie is standing there thinking to his self thirty days. So Robbie goes on saying Pebbles has children who is going to care for her children. She had left the kids here with me you see. One of her daughters father had picked her up and has had her for a couple of days. So I just have one of her kids. Mrs. Truman just said quickly when Sandra calls you. You can talk to her about the kids and you and her can make some kind of arrangments from there. And Mrs. Truman told Robbie to have a nice day and she hung up the phone. Robbie is walking around the house like he had lost his mind and he's looking for it. But really he is looking for Pebbles mom phone number and can't remember where he had put it at. Well finally he found it and he's thinking and dialing the phone number. He is hoping that she will be nicer this time. Oh well the phone is ringing and Mrs. Cook answer's the phone. Robbie takes a deep breath and he says hi Mrs. Cook this is Robbie and he went on saying Pebbles boyfriend. And than he quickly start saying that your daughter is at the bendigo rehab for women. A Mrs. Truman had call me and said that she only gets one phone call a day. And there is no visiting days there at all. Pebbles mom is very quiet and she is just listening to make sure she gets all the information correctly. And she didn't hold a conversation with him at all. She just says thank you and hangs up the phone. Well Robbie is relieve that he got that over with. And now he can sit and wait for Pebbles to call. Not knowing what to say but one thing he know he's going to let her know. The shit she pulled was fuck up.

CHAPTER 7

REALITY FOR PEBBLES

The dusky smell in the air a little mildew smell similar to a toilet smell. Pebbles is sitting in her room they had given her. And there is another person in there. Pebbles was not in the no talking mood. She's feeling weak, very weak not getting any rest for over a week. She's sitting there wondering what is being said about her. Really she just wants to disappear off the face of the world. Thats what crack heads do go and hide when coming down off the high. A guilt that takes place of the addiction. Being high no worries all the problems you had was there but now going. Thats what crack does control your mind. Robbie is now home waiting for his phone call from Pebbles. He have been going over in his head what he's going to say. And really he didn't get it together what it is yet. But he had decided he's not going to be nice at all. And why be nice to her she's playing me as a fool and these days. A good black man is hard to find. Robbie is really anxious for the phone to ring. And finally the phone rings and yes it is Pebbles on the other end of the phone. Robbie is picking up the phone almost dropping the phone handle. And the only thing is coming out of his mouth is Pebbles is that you. Yo! Pebbles. And the other end of the phone is Pebbles. And now Pebbles is saying Robbie calm down why did you drop the phone. Who the hell you got in my damn house. Robbie is saying to his self she has alot of damn nerve. Hey Pebbles, Robbie getting out what he has rehearsal all morning. You know that was fuck up what you did. Don't say shit until I'm finish. You just do what you want and think it's alright. Your fat ass girlfriend Martha been here and I put her ass out. In here talking shit. And if you want to know since you haven't asked your kids is fine and their health is good. Since the crack seems to have made you forget all about them. Now Robbie is getting real loud and now the last thing. I have to say your little friend came here looking for you. And he said that you stole his pack. And he didn't say that he was going to whoop your ass or anything. But he said that you owe him one now nigger what the fuck that means. At this time Pebbles is not saying anything you could hear her crying through the phone. And she's trying to get out her words but she's crying so hard they wont come out. Now Robbie is feeling sorry that he had holler so he's just saying. Baby don't cry everything is going to be alright. The people in there is going to help you ok! ok! baby. And Pebbles says in a very weak voice ok. And then she just says thank you Robbie for everything. I will talk to you tomorrow and I will call when the girls are there. Ok bye and she hangs up. Now Robbie is feeling good he got out what he felt. But just feeling bad that Pebbles has a real serious problem. A problem that he can't fix. The thirty days in bendigo for Pebbles was rough and hard. She had to deal with issues that was hard alot to do with the fathers of her kids that left her. She talked about her own father and that she don't think he loves her. And she know that she has to face reality. Her family and Robbie and the girls getting back home was hard. Pebbles mom was visiting alot she would come and visit and don't know when to leave. Tia was back home and Bruce told

Pebbles try leaving his daughter like that again and he is going to take her to court. And he told her that he is going to win. Pebbles knows what she did was wrong and she felt so bad about it. She didn't go out much just to the welfare bank and her mom would take her. All her girlfriends and people she knew didn't have much to say to her at all. Pebbles mom would be standing there holding her bible in her hand. But her mom and sister thinks its easy to stop doing drugs. The pressure for Pebbles being reminded all the time about her faults was not good for her. Pebbles sister Donna would call and check up on her. But really the conversation was all about Donna and how well her life is going. But Pebbles just listens.

CHAPTER 8

PEBBLES

Well getting back home and dealing with my mom. Something I took and I try not to tell what was on my mind. Because it wasn't nice that she was treating me like a damn child. She was coming into my house, my house and was running things. I got tired and told her to go over there with her husband and drive him crazy. My mom's wanted to argue and tell me. I wanted to go back and do drugs. Well I simply said you make someone want to do drugs. I guess my mom wanted me to feel guilty. And I was just sick and tired of feeling gulity. My mom had walked up stairs to use the bathroom. And she left her pocketbook on the floor. I had took her wallet out and took all the money out. I know she's going to be real upset when she finds it missing. But what the hell I'm going to get high tonight. My mom comes back down stairs and she looks at me. I'm not saying nothing. I just want her to leave. Here she goes with her mouth again. Damn! can she just get out of my house. And if she looks in her pocketbook. I'm not giving back her money to her. Whatever she is saying I don't hear her. My heart is beating real fast and my mind is just set on a hit. And she will not leave. Mom get out of my house now in a tone of voice like if I was her mother. My mom walks to the door and turns around. And she's says I'm leaving your house and walks out the door. Pebbles mom getting into her car and cannot believe that she put her out like that. Pebbles mom was not in the rush to get home. She pulls up to Mac Donalds drive thru and she order a big mac combo. And then she drives up to the window to pay for it. She looks in her pocketbook no money in her wallet. The little young girl is at the window with the order and her hand is out for the money. Without a word she drives off real fast. Now! Pebbles mom is burning up hot. Just saying to herself over and over again. I don't believe this! That damn girl took my money. Now she know she's living dangerous messing with my pocketbook. I'm not going over there because someone is going to jail and it will not be me. Well Pebbles went back to being Pebbles and she didn't let nothing get in her way. Robbie had started back staying out all night long. Pebbles putting him out every other night. And Pebbles had went back to having her wild parties at night. And they are wild Martha, Yonnie and Danielle they be putting their thing down. Music going on full blast most of the time the kids is upstairs looking at t.v. And someone from the party be checking up on them. Coming in the room just talking real nice. No food in the house and that had just started to be a everyday thing. The only time Tia and Shayla have a meal is in school and they be hungry. One day Tia had called her grandmother and asked her grandmom can her and Shayla come and live there. Pebbles mom had went to the school and had pick the girls up. And Pebbles had no ideal and was it drama going on. Yes! Pebbles mom and the child protective service had made a visit at the home. Pebbles answer the door and steps outside to talk to the lady and her mom. Pebbles mom steps in her face in front of the door. And she ask her to move they are going in there. Pebbles states clearly this is my house and they going to need the police. Because that's the only way they were getting in there. So child protective brought an officer back to complete the investigation. Pebbles was ready for them she clean the whole house from top to bottom. And she made her friends leave and she asked them to stay away for a couple of days or so. She also went out and made some fast money from the streets to buy some food. She is sitting there talking and she knows what to say and how to say it. And then she turns to her mother and said real nicely please bring back my daughters. They are my kids not yours. The worker and the officer said they don't have a problem letting her children back into the home. Tia and Shayla comes back home. Pebbles realized that her children is going to get her in alot of trouble. And thats something she doesn't need at all. Pebbles loves getting high and no one is not going to get in her way. Everyday Pebbles is hollering telling Tia and Shayla. Whatever happens in this house stays in this house. And if someone asks them anything she simply told the kids to tell them to ask their mom. If they want to know anything. Pebbles is busy trying to deal with the school and her mom. Robbie and his cheating ways, fighting all the time with him.

CHAPTER 9

TIA

I am just nine years old and it seems that I'm older than that. My mom acts like a mom only when she wants too. And thats not all the time at all. My mom makes simple things she make it seems so hard to do. And always have excuse's why something is not done. Our house is not dirty that something someone on the outside would say. Because all the people that comes in and out all day and night. Every-day my mom reminds me what to do and how to act when I'm away from home. Because she said I was not going to get her in trouble no more. I just don't say nothing when she is preaching. Robbie does not get in my mom's way at all. My mom had just announce that she is having another baby. I wonder how it is going to be like having a new baby in the house. Is my mom going to change, I'm just hoping things will get better. But I'm only nine years old and I will be ten years old soon. When my grandmother heard the news the only thing she says is OH MY GOD! What is that girl doing having another baby. But my mom acts like she's a queen sitting on top of a hill or something. Robbie had went out and got a job. Every pay-day he would buy food and alot of things for the house. But my mom said she rather have the money in her hand. And if she wants those things she would buy them herself. Robbie would tell her that his baby is on the way soon. And he don't want to hear it. But I know why my mom wants the money in her hand. Everything had started to get better. Robbie had stop all the wild parties. When he is home from work he is like a guard at the door waiting for somebody to knock on the door. He told my mom that while she is pregnant no partying. And thats when the fights begin. My mom would say no one is stopping her from doing what she wants. The baby in her stomach don't stop nothing she would holler real loud. Robbie had said OH YEAH! And he called the child protective service on my mom. Now its a social worker comes around and a visiting nurse. The worker would take me in another room and talk to me alone. But I don't say nothing. I like it when my dad comes and picks me up. I be having so much fun alot of times I don't want to go back home at all. But my sister Shayla would be by herself. Robbie he has made everything much better since there's a baby on the way. Everybody is happy but my mom. She tells Robbie that black people don't know how to act when they get money. And she always telling Robbie so what your working. I'm so happy that Robbie is there even thou my mom is not happy. Because things is not going her way.

CHAPTER 10

PEBBLES IS PREGNANT

I'm pregnant again but this time I'm not alone with this baby. When Robbie heard the news he was happy. He was trying to all of sudden change me. No man tells Pebbles what to do. Robbie went out job hunting and he found a nice full-time job. I wasn't all that happy like he was because he should of that before I gotten pregnant. He was buying food on pay-day fixing up the house. He even brought new furniture. Fix the kids bedroom up in Barbie everything. But he will not give me any money in my hand. So everything Robbie did he just had did it. And I didn't have a smile on my face at all. He didn't want nobody in the house while he was at work. And I was cussing and fussing because I wanted to do what I wanted to do. I didn't want the nice things he was offering. I wanted my life to not change. It's nothing wrong about drinking and smoking crack because everyone is doing it. Robbie was not stoping me at all. So I would leave and do my business else where. He takes and call my mom telling her everything. Like thats going to change my mind. He acts like he never smoke crack before. He is a in the closet type. But one thing I can say he didn't make smoking a habit at all. Robbie my Robbie is a momma's boy. Robbie always makes it clear that he is never going to leave me. No matter what happens or the fuck up things I does. He is not going to leave yell but he always says that but always out there cheating. He is cheating with this one and that one. But I know! I'm the bitch holding the cards. I'm having his baby and he's taking care of my girls. And he's fixing up my house. So the bitch's out there is just being played for real. And I'm not worried at all, I'm just living one day at a time. Because I told Robbie that he don't want me to come and look for him. Well child protective service showed up at my door. And was I surprise for real. Someone called and said that I'm pregnant and using drugs. I let them in because the house is looking nice now. But I know Robbie had called them. Damn! he makes me so sick. So I talked to the worker and I did not tell her, I'm using drugs at all. I think she thought I was going to tell her that. Shit I'm not stupid. I have been dealing with these white people since Shayla been a baby. And I already know the routine that goes with it. She does notice that I'm six months almost seven months pregnant. She asks me what was my plans for the new baby. And I told her that I was taking care of it like I'm doing for my daughters. The worker was sitting there with a kind of straight face. She ask me can see where the kids sleep at. With a smirk on my face I was happy to take her to their bedroom. Tia and Shayla room is laid out in Barbie everything. They has a desk with a lamp on it and that is also Barbie. The worker was kind of shock but she shouldn't be. Because my house is fixed up in new stuff. Robbie says that he is buying the girls a t.v. for their bedroom. The worker had told me that since someone had called an complaint on me. That she has to investigate as always thats what happens. But I'm not worried because I'm cutting down on everything until my baby gets here. The worker had left and said she will keep in contact. So that means that she can pop up at the door at anytime. Damn! Because my phone is disconnected and the cable is disconnected also. Those are my bills to pay and I didn't pay them so they are off. Just that! I try to keep myself so calm. But one thing I know that Robbie had called them people. And he walks around like he didn't call them. It's alright thou Robbie brought everything for the baby. The bassinet is so pretty but; I'm not use to nice things like that. And in shock! Robbie had started telling me he loves me. But I never says nothing back. Because I don't love him the only man I love is my daddy. I had cut down on the drugs. But I guess Robbie thinks I'm going to stop for good. Because the baby is coming he is taking care of his baby and if he needs day care to go to work. It's gonna have to be that way. I am Pebbles.

CHAPTER 11

ROBBIE IS A DADDY

Robbie is hollering! Pebbles everything is going to be alright. Robbie holding her hand Pebbles snatchs her hand back. Pebbles is in labor and never had anyone there before. When she was giving birth to Tia and Shayla. Robbie saying baby I love you and you can do it. Pebbles is not wanting to hear nothing the contractions is three minutes apart. Awww! Pebbles is hollering Oh My God! Pebbles telling Robbie go and get the nurse of doctor. Get them in here Robbie had went and got the nurse. And Pebbles is asking her how long will be until delivery. And the nurse is telling her that it will not be long. And that the doctor will be in soon. At this time Robbie is sweating trying to hold Pebbles hand. The doctors had came in and it was time to go in the delivery room. For the baby to arrive they got Pebbles set up to go in the delivery room. Robbie had to put on a gown and prepared to go in. In the delivery room the doctor says, It's a girl. Robbie is so happy and Pebbles finally has a big smile on her face. Oh she's so pretty Pebbles is saying. The baby is here and Pebbles is in her room. Her and Robbie is calling the whole family on each side. It was a girl weighing six pounds and six ounces. And her name is Robin Nia

Cook. Robbie had named her. His mother and family came out to the hospital with alot of baby stuff for Robin. With all the excitement and it was so crowded. With everyone coming to see the baby. In a sudden shock! I heard someone say hey baby girl my daddy voice. Pebbles saying daddy you came to see me. With a tear drop in my eye Pebbles is in a moment like if she was dreaming. She said you see your grand daughter. Another one I hope the next one is a boy. My mother is smiling and seems so happy. Getting back home me and the new baby. Robbie would do everything for Robin. And she had the cutest outfits and so much stuff. I had realized I did have a good man finally. Robbie was working his ass off and bringing home the pay check. My house was looking great and soon I had start to change my ways. Tia and Shayla was happy and especially with their baby sister. They would make stuff at school and bring it home for Robin. I had stop doing what I wanted and stop the partying. Well I wasn't use to nice things. Well shit a good man like Robbie don't come in my life every-day. Martha, Yonnie and Danielle would come and visit but they all know. I have a good thing going on now. I would tell them I'm getting my shit together. I have a family now and you know how your so called girlfriends act when you doing better than they are. They talk about all the bad things they can think of about you. Because they don't have anything to say bad about you at that time. Well I didn't care what they had said, shoot I was living good. My girls had got their own t.v. and I got my cable turn on and the telephone. And I pays the bill every month when my money comes. Robin she looks just like Robbie and she loves her daddy. And in a million years I never thought I would be so happy. Especially with another man besides Big-Cal. But since I had been going to my meetings. I'm starting to understand the addiction. And getting high is not worth losing my man and children. I had started going to school and I had put

Robin in day-care. Oh she started getting so big and she has the prettiest smile. She was always grinning. Tia had did a speech in school and it was about her family. And in her speech that had brought tears to my eyes. She said her mom was so special to her that her mother she looks up to when she is sad. Her mother is like a butterfly that is so fragile to her. In her speech she said her family is not rich and they are not poor. But love is much richer. Me and Robbie and Shayla and the new baby. We all is sitting in the audience that made me feel good. Staying clean wasn't easy actually a struggle. But to try to stay clean wasn't hard as I thought it would be. I guess in the past I didn't want to get cleaned and help. But going to my meetings now I get up and talk about the days getting high. And what I had accomplished in my life now. Seven months had past by and none of my girlfriends does not never come and visit. When passing them by in the streets me and my children. The bitchs have the nerve to roll their eyes looking all bad. And their not getting no where in life. Well I just say hi and keep stepping. Because Pebbles holds her head up high. Robbie had went out and brought a new car well used but it's just like new. Me and Robbie and the kids goes everywhere now. My sister Donna calls me but she don't have much to say. Because I always tells her my life is straight as a line. Now what can Donna Cook say now.

CHAPTER 12

PEBBLES

It's a year now and my baby girl now is a year old. And everything so wonderful and being clean never could believe a whole year. Having problems but nothing Pebbles cannot deal with at all. Robbie got all kinds of women out there. Even got my daughter around those bitchs like I don't know. But Pebbles know whats going on. Robbie staying out all night long nothing with him had change. Just the fact he is working and doing things a man should do. Taking care of his family at home. I'm dealing with my problems I had and it's hard at times. Taking care of my daughters and Robbie is always telling me if it wasn't for him. I wouldn't had stop getting high. BULL SHIT! And that's bull-shit for real. After giving birth to Robin, I notice alot of good things Robbie had done. And alot of things I never had or a man never gave me but sex you know. I gave in an said I was going to do the right thing. I'm clean but how long, I don't know. Robbie is walking over top of me. I no longer have any girlfriends but I do still consider them as my girls. Even thou they don't come around to see me. Yes! I miss them. Well I miss alot of things but I have to continue keeping things looking good. My mom and dad is very proud of me and I want to keep it that way. I still goes to my meetings and the meetings keep me strong. I can talk about my problems now. And what I am going through of staying clean. Sometimes I have dreams of partying and getting high. And in my dream I'm looking for my lighter to light my pipe. But cannot find a lighter to fire it up. I had told everybody in the meeting about my dreams. And alot of them said they all been there. And the dreams are natural to have. It's something crack does to your brain. So the meetings makes me strong and keep me clean. Because I know I'm not by myself at all. The things I done in the past I'm not proud of and I'm just Pebbles. But being clean makes me feel so different and so weak. Tia and Shayla knows about me going to meetings to get better. Tia is eleven years old and smart as a wit. She tells me mom please don't start back drinking ok. But I'm fighting and it's one day at a time. No one knows it's not easy at all. He just wants me sitting in the house waiting on him. He's working and taking care of me so he's always telling me why should I worry. That's a damn man for you. A man who wants their cake and eat it too. But I takes a deep breath to calm my nerves. Because I know! I will be brought up on some charges. All the anger thats under my skin. I'm doing the right thing and he is not changing for me. Now he's got money of his own. I want to put him out of my house and then he might take all the furniture. And then Robin would really miss her daddy. She is walking and saying her first words. So I'm living a one day at a time thing here. Dealing with shit day after day here in the hood. I'm hoping and praying to stay clean for me and the children.

CHAPTER 13

PEBBLES

Martha came and visit and I was so surprise. And yes nervous I was. She was telling me everything what is going on in the hood. And how all the players was asking about me. And I smile putting my head down. Forgetting about I'm in recovery. Martha was looking tore up thou or is that I'm just noticing it just now. And then she started telling me about Danielle. And her sneaky ass was out there tricking to get high. I shouldn't never had let her fat ass in my house. Because I didn't need to hear about the people and what they are doing. But it feels like I'm trap in a jail cell. And I'm not free to be Pebbles. I was the one who made the rules. I did what I wanted and when I wanted. And now I got a damn man having me sitting in this damn house. What is I'm going to lose and what is I'm going to gain. I'm not happy yell in the meetings they tell us going through recovery. We are sometimes not going to be happy. But damn this is not me at all. I don't love Robbie I'm just being someone I'm not. I'm on the inside looking on the outside at everyone who is free as a bird. Tears is running down Pebbles face. Robin walks up to Pebbles and she picks her up holding her and rocking her. Until Pebbles wakes up holding

Robin in her arms. And the first thought came to her mind. I almost went back to getting high again. I almost went back damn. Robbie haven't came home yet he is playing with me or something. Pebbles got up and put Robin in her crib. Walked to the window looking out and a tear drop roll out one of her eyes. She started talking to herself saying to herself saying God please help me to be strong its hard. Why me, why me. And tears started rolling down more and more. Someone had walked in it was Robbie. He walked over to Pebbles and said baby I'm sorry I'm late. And he had pulled her to him and held her tight. For the first time in years Pebbles had felt safe. Just Robbie touch some how made her feel good. But as he was holding her she needed more than being held. Because her body is aching. Being in recovery the meetings and everything. The people who come to the meetings. They all want to be your friend. But I feel like this I don't have time smiling in people face. Because black people don't know how to mind their business. It's enough coming to the meetings and staying clean. It's hard but I missed everything and if I said. I didn't missed everything well its not the truth. But if I pray hard enough I know I can make it. Living in the ghetto a place for the poor people thats how I look at it. And if you see white people living in the ghetto. Because they are considered as white trash well I had heard all that in my meetings. Because we do have white people in there and they called them selfs that. Well I was out food shopping because food stamps came out. And it seems like all the black folks is in the same place at the same time. Happy everybody is happy. Everybody man is with them holding hands pushing shopping carts. I just called that day Mothers Day. It's me and the kids out shopping and I was looking good. Well I was in the line to get waited on to get up and out of there. It was one older lady behind me and behind her shopping cart. Was two females from around the way. So I'm standing there minding my business and from no where. I over heard both females talking about me. Saying yell the bitch use to smoke crack. I kindly excuse myself leaning over the older women shopping cart. I had pointed my finger at them saying. I know you bitchs is not talking about me. Well Pebbles going to give you something to talk about to your man when you get home. I had both of your men in bed that's right. Neither one of them did not say a word. Because Pebbles was loud and didn't care who had heard her. Pebbles paid for her food with her food stamps. She started pushing her shopping cart she looks back at both females smiling. Well Pebbles didn't know the two girls but she knew their man real well.

CHAPTER 14

PROBLEMS

I'm clean and still attending my meetings. I had started seeing a change in Shayla. She started acting up in school and with the teachers. She had just turn nine years old and it seems that all problems had started with her. Thats when I had to be extra strong. I had caught her smoking my cigarettes my damn cigarettes at that. I would just talk to her but in the worse way. I wanted to woop her little ass for real. Shayla would call me names in my face. I couldn't take it and the teachers keep calling everyday. It had got to the point I will not answer the phone certain times of the day. But shit teachers calls at night like its something that their job required. Shayla knows that her father is not interested of being her father. Even thou he is always in jail all the time. And it hurts that he threw me away and his daughter. Yes it hurts like hell, But we live and learn from our mistakes. And when I go to school to talk to teachers and counslers. They give me this look when I tells them all three kids have all different fathers and it's the truth. Shit! I know some women who have seven kids and seven fathers to go along with it. Well Shayla have alot of problems just being nine years old. And I'm trying to deal with her. I don't ask

Robbie to be there as a father because she already has one. And why bother black men these days don't take care of other men kids. And thats something I know for a fact. They are just there and if they can get a free ride they are going to ride. Well going to the meetings it was getting to be easy because most of the time. I didn't say much it had started to get stressful at home with Shayla. And Robbie started acting strange lately and I just can't put my finger on it. But it's something, I just know it. All of sudden he wants to keep the house clean. And he is even in the kitchen cooking the meals. I'm like saying to myself. Damn! Whats up. Dealing with Shayla and all her talking back to me. It seems she is really out of control or it's just she hates me or something. Well it was like six in the morning and everyone is sound of sleep. So while everything is quiet I decided to sit on the stoop outside the door. To just think and get fresh air at the same time. So as I was sitting there I thought I seen something on Robbie's car. Because it was blowing laying flat on the car and then back up. So I gets up and walked to the car. And damn if it wasn't a note and it says **Robbie your daughter Rashell needs pampers**. No name at the end of the note or anything. And was I mad! I was over beyond mad I was just telling myself. Pebbles calm down calm down girl. So what I did I waited right outside with the note in my hand. I'm waiting for Robbie goes to get in the car to leave for work. And I will be sitting here waiting yes. Yes the time has come here comes Robbie coming out the door and he walks by me going to the car. He did not see me at all. And I gets up and walked right over there with the note. And I taps him on the shoulder he turns around. Here's your note. I'm hitting him saying you got a damn baby out there. Now I'm screaming, I'm sitting here in this damn house everyday and you out there making babies. Robbie is holding his hands up towards his head. Pebbles is really hollering now. A baby name Rashell and yell thats why you been to damn extra nice to me. Robbie had never had got the car door unlock because he is pushed up on the car. With Pebbles not moving out of the way. Pebbles step back and said go in the house and get all of your shit and I mean all of it. Oh Player! Just your clothes OK! And go the fuck with who ever you got a baby with. Pebbles is hollering! Robbie just go ok. Robbie got all of his stuff that she had allowed him to get. I didn't even allowed him to kiss Robin good bye. He had just got out of my way and left.

CHAPTER 15

NO MAN FOR PEBBLES

Well it wasn't the same without my man around. I just know that something that looks good is not good. When a man treats you to good. And all of sudden he puts a crown on your head as the queen of the world. Something is wrong I had stayed in bed for like a whole week. I didn't go to no meetings I was really down and out. And getting back to myself and all alone again. I didn't have much to say to my mother. And when my sister Donna calls I just didn't say much at all. Well at first I didn't say nothing to no one about what had happen. I know one thing Robin really miss her daddy. She walks from room to room looking for him. She goes to the front door looking out to see if he's coming up the walk way. Well I had to get back to myself and start looking good. I had not even try to do anything to my hair pulled it back. Just like when I was out there smoking crack. And thats something I didn't want to think about at all. Now it has been two weeks and Robbie haven't try to call or nothing at all. Well I guess he's with his new baby that he made behind my back. Right now I'm thinking what I could of would things now. But he was wrong for real and then he have a nerve to start being extra nice.

That's what blew his secret for real. Well I'm getting back to being Pebbles. I don't have any girlfriends that don't get high. And I'm clean for over a year now what do I have in common with my old friends. But I need to go to a meeting real quick. Before I do go back to the world. Back to my meetings getting a ride was hard. But I would beg my mom and dad for rides. And most of the time I would just walked home and I be so tired. Tia and Shayla and the baby Robin. Martha would baby sit in my house not that I wanted it that way. But I had to go to my meetings and Martha she's nice to help. And she would say Pebbles you are really getting yourself together for real. And that was so nice to say. But I really I was weak and I needed Robbie. And I was missing him for real. It has been a month and here comes Robbie knocking on the door. I opens the door and here he goes saying he miss Robin. So I says in a smart way. You do huh! I lets him in and Robin was so happy to see him. Only thing I can do is smile but I know he's not staying. Well he had only stayed for thirty minutes WOW! So as he was leaving to go back to the car. And what do I see a baby car sit in the back sit of the car. And yes I snap out. I had punched Robbie like if he was a punching bag. Yes I did. He was saying I was crazy girl you are crazy. And I was yelling back. Damn right I'm crazy nigger. Neighbors had broke us up. And Robbie had got in his car and drove away. I don't know why men play with us. I really don't know. I'm still going to my meetings but not really going all the time like I should. Well walking home from one of my meetings a old school friend name Kareem Ali gave me a ride. He stop and said Pebbles do you need a ride. I had turned around and said huh but then I notice who it was now my heart is beating real fast. Because I use to like him in high school. Well I gets in the car and the car is sharp and smelling real good too. Oh my God this is what I'm saying to myself. I'm nervous for real one part I does remember is that he don't have a girlfriend. And I had said to myself Yes! As Kareem taking me home at last I was feeling that there is hope after all. Kareem is a fine brother he is fine as wine. And yes I invited him in the house. Martha had a look on her face like where did she pick him up at. And then Martha had said hi damn you look good. Pebbles is standing there smiling saying to Martha girl it's time to go. Thank you for baby sitting. And I did not waste anytime getting him in the bed at all. The same night exactly and it was great. With Kareem in my life things were looking better for me. And I wasn't thinking about Robbie at all. But it was one thing I was worried about Kareem finding out about my past. And I say past because it's been over a year now. That I have not used any drugs or drank and I had clean up real good to have use to be a crack head. So everyday I pray and hope that Kareem doesn't find out. It just seems like I'm walking on pins everyday. And when he comes to spend time with me it's just like I'm in heaven. I had always liked Kareem in school. I even found myself day dreaming and yes I was a teen. And in those days girls did not approach the guys at all. I never went out to much back then. My mom was the one who came out and find you where ever your at. She was the typed mother that didn't wait until you got in like the other mothers. She will come looking for you and get you in the house. So I never went out to much because I know I had a limit. So everything I done I had very much did as an adult. When Robbie found out some other player laying in his bed chilling. He did not like it at all but so what. I knew he was going to find out. Because people always talking about everybody else business. But I did not care. But then again I had started caring. Because someone told my man Kareem Ali about my past. And it hit me like fire crackers. And the news about my pregnancy. Whew!

CHAPTER 16

PREGNANT

I'm thirty years old and pregnant and all alone again. Kareem found out about everything and he left me. Yes he left me on the spot. Yes I told him that I was having his baby. He did not care he told me that he did not like all the stuff he heard. It was just too much for him. Damn, I was hurt not only hurt-crush. So enough is enough and I took my yellow ass back on the streets and I didn't care at all. When Robbie found out he came back home. Because I blames everything on him and he just keeps telling me how sorry he is. But all his sorry's was just too late. I'm crack out and pregnant and he know's it's not his baby. Shayla everyday is getting into more and more trouble. It's alot to cope with. I had started selling our stuff out of the house to get high. And I really think everyone wanted me to go down. Robbie was in and out as usual. I'm almost seven months and I don't even look like it at all. Kareem came and visit me once during the pregnancy . He had gave me a phone number to call when I have the baby. He told me shaking his head that I looked a mess. The comment had hurt but it was the truth. I had just took the phone number and he left. I know that I wont know where the phone number is when the baby comes. So I had called my mom and gave it to her for me to have when the time comes. My mom is not really talking to me. So what, thats what I say. Shit its hard to stay clean. Child protective service is back on my ass again. Shayla have been caught stealing in three stores. And only thing I does is go and get her. Not even talking to her telling her thats wrong to steal. Because I'm busy out there doing wrong myself. Tia she stays out of my way. Alot of times I wonder whats going on with her. Because she doesn't talk at all. Bruce comes and get her on the weekends but she will be with her father the whole summer. So it will be just me and that bad ass daughter of mine Shayla and shes a handful. I mostly leaves Robin with her father once he's home from work. So I know he don't have time for the bitch and his other baby. But he tells me I got alot of nerve and pregnant with another man's baby. A man who does not want you. But I learned to laugh at the things that hurt me. As I got older it becomes easy. Well I had got high up to the day of delivery and I didn't care at all. The doctors thought I was crazy for being on drugs during pregnancy. Oh they had asked about 100 questions and they said that I'm in alot of trouble. I did not care at all not this time. Because they don't know the pain I was feeling. Kareem he hurt me so bad and he left me and he didn't care. But he did leave his phone number to call when I does have the baby. And I look at it like this he must just want the baby. But he's going to have to take it because the state is taking the baby. The hospital is making sure of it and I don't care. Because when I get out of here I'm going home and get my smoke on just like that. Why should I care about this cold, cold world. Robbie was out there in the hall way wanting to come in the labor room. But I told the nurses that I wanted nobody in there with me. I was in alot of pain but only if the doctor can help me with something for the pain. But the doctor just came in to check how far I have to go. He told me that it was better to have it natural. Because all the drugs thats already in my blood. I just want this baby to come now. Damn I'm hurting so bad please baby come. Pebbles is holding her belly rocking back and forth. Finally it's time to have the baby. There is silence in there I'm worried whats going on. The doctors is moving fast preparing the equipment. Now it's time to push I'm pushing but my pushing is not enough. I'm saying to myself oh my God. The baby must be dead and now the doctors is asking me to give a final push the baby is coming. I started pushing and here it comes finally the baby is out. And all I was listening out for was a cry. I heard the baby cry thats all I wanted to hear. And it was a girl weighing just five pounds. Well finally after all the doctors had to sew and all the other things they do. I was put in a regular room and I called my mom to tell her about the baby. But she already knew because Robbie already had call her and told her that I was having the baby. I had asked for the baby's father phone number and she had given it to me. And it wasn't much to say at this point about anything. So I had thanked my mom and I hung up. I had called Kareem on the phone a female had answer the phone. She said he was there and she handed him the phone. I started out real low talking but I said Kareem the baby is here. It's a girl and I had named her Karen. At first I don't hear anything and then he said that he was coming out to the hospital to pick up the baby. And that he does not want me in his baby's life at all. And he hung up the phone. With tears in my eyes I had laid there looking at my baby. For the last time.

CHAPTER 17

TIA

I was 14 years old leaving home. My mom had never stop doing drugs after giving birth to my baby sister Karen. Well nobody seen her but my mom. Because the baby father came to the hospital and pick her up. And my mom had got worse smoking and drinking. I had never really said anything. But through the years the kids tease me and beat me up. Well I left because it wasn't the need to be there any longer. My mom looks had went down hill from all the drugs. And she wasn't as attractive to the guys that sells the drugs or to any man. Well it was a day that my mom didn't have no money. And the young dude he was about 17 or 18 years old. I don't know really how old but she was down stairs begging for drugs. And the young dude had told her that he wouldn't touch her even if he had gloves on. She kept begging so I didn't hear anymore talking. So my guess he left but he didn't. Only thing I know he was standing in my bedroom giving me a look. And oh was I scared he said your mom sent me up here. She owes me a favor and it's you. I was trying to run out of the room. But he had grab me and threw me on the bed. I started screaming he had slap me so hard that my whole body became numb. And he did what he came in there to do. After everything and I mean everything I had got up barely walking. I had got up and I had got all my clothes it wasn't much at all. And I left and I was not coming back. I had one friend and it was my girlfriend Beth. My only friend and she was white no one black in school wanted to be my friend at all. But her and me we had click for real. I had walked to her house and it was a walk but I had made it there. My feet was hurting, hurting wasn't the word. Her mom and dad said that I was welcome to stay there as long as I want. Well it end up till I had graduate from high school. And the funny thing about it my mom never came looking for me. And my dad Bruce he knew that I was staying with my girlfriend. And he didn't have a problem with it at all. I always stayed looking nice with my grayish eyes and my very light complexion. Things had went well for me at times I did think about Shayla and my sister Robin that I had left behind. Living with Beth and her family it showed me a different side of life. I did hear that Shayla was on drugs real heavy. And when hearing that my sister had to be like 15 years old. After graduating from high school I had got a job at a bank. I always did my work and did it carefully. All my bank customers they all liked me. I was a bank teller and the good thing about it. No one from the ghetto never came in there. I never talks about my mother and sisters to no one. That was something I had put behind me. I had got a beautiful apartment in the surburban area where it wasn't many blacks. And that had became my hiding place. I had manage to get a boyfriend and he's name is Andrew. When I met him I fell in love that kind of love that makes a sister smile everyday. Andrew mother had accepted me right away. And that had made me feel so good. She had asked about my mother and I had told her that my mother had passed away when I was a baby. It was kind of good that his parents accepted me and I am black. And I didn't want to mess things up for me at all. Even thou I'm 18 years old. I am still out here alone. But Beth is always there for me on holidays thru the years especially Christmas. Beth parents will have a big Christmas party and all of the decorations and lights. It was so beautiful and then somewhere the memory's from a little girl will come in my mind. With very little present's and no food in the house. Looking at the beautiful lights reality comes back. Well I feel like this it is easy to forget than to remember. And I had made up in my mind a long time ago that I was not coming back. To where I left behind. My relationship with Andrew is a dream come true lots of romantic dinners. After work the candles lit and with slow music that comes with it. It feels like heaven when I'm with him. Ok my life is perfect a beautiful apartment and a nice paying job. And all I need is my past to stay where it is. I been through alot as a little girl and I seen alot of things. That little girls should have never seen. And if I have to repeat my child hood again. I wouldn't want to live it not one day. I'm working everyday and having time for my man Andrew everyday. Until one day I came home from work and my apartment is broken into my TV and VCR is stolen. Now at this time I am thinking while the police is in my apartment doing an investigation. Damn! I'm saying who will come and break into my place. Andrew came to give me support that I needed. I would never think something like that would happen in that neighborhood. Only where I came from the ghetto. I had replace the items that was taken and I continue with my life. But every once in a while I would still think who will do something like that to me. Now its one year from now and my life is still the same but one thing different. Andrew had proposed to me oh my heart drops. And I had said yes. Andrew my man my soon to be husband. He had moved in so everything was perfect. I was rushing inside my apartment and one of the neighbors that I barely ever talk too. She had said that my sister was here looking for you. And in shock! I said what sister and oh I'm so happy Andrew was not home yet. She said yes your sister Shayla. So I did not say nothing. I had just let her talk to see what was going on. Well she goes and say that she had knock on her door. And she had introduced herself to her as Shayla and that she was my sister. I had cut the lady off from what she was going to say. Look I don't have a sister ok. So I suggested that if that young lady knocks on your door. You should call the cops ok, I had gave her smile and told her to have a good day. I goes in my apartment and shut the door. And at this time I'm sweating. And I'm standing there with tears coming down my face how did they find me. Tia is now trying to get herself together before Andrew comes home. I'm not saying nothing to Andrew but if Shayla or mom knocks on this door. I am acting like I don't know them and I will call the cops. I does not go messing with them. A month have passed and no one came there knocking. But one day after work I comes home someone again had broke into my apartment again. And this time alot of my clothes, TV my VCR. Andrew stereo and his lap top computer. I had called the cops again my neighbor had came over and wanted to come in. I had let her in and she told me the girl who knock on her door. She had seen her moving my stuff out. Her and a older lady and a man. Now at this time I'm hot burning up. I ask her trying to calm myself down in front of the cops. I said you didn't call the police. And she says I didn't want trouble they look kind of rough. So one of the cops had took her to the side and talk to her. Now everything is coming to me the first time must was them. Now why did they come back and get caught. Now how dumb is that oh they are going to jail for real. And I know the older lady was my mom but I cannot prove that. But Shayla is going to jail because she has been seen. I had never told Andrew about who broke into our apartment. We had replace everything that was taken. Shayla did go to jail and my mom never did go to jail. And she never came back here messing with me at all. Me and Andrew had got married a big wedding. With his family and my friend Beth and her family. It was all in sparklin white, I felt like an princess. Andrew was my family my only family.

CHAPTER 18

PEBBLES (THE END)

After giving birth to Karen my life had went down hill and it never came back up. I had started looking real bad and I gotten to the point that I did not care. Robbie never stayed home and he always took Robin with him. I had made my home a drop stop crack house. Tia had left home my guess is that she's living with her daddy and she can stay there. As far as children Shayla had started doing everything. And she even started doing drugs and drinking. Shit! Shayla was partying harder than I was. She didn't have problems getting high because she was young. When I found out that she was actually smoking crack. I had went off on her telling her she had lost her damn mind. I was screaming you see where these drugs got me at. You see these drugs got me looking ugly. Shayla is this what you want. And only thing Shayla could say is that my girlfriends that I hang with told her to try it. And stop smoking weed all the time. I'm standing there saying my girlfriends. Damn of all people and they see the girl was already trouble from the start. And trouble thats what everyone is going to get. And as for me I couldn't stop her at all. Robbie had left me alone when he found out that Shayla was a little smoker.

And he took Robin with him. It seems that I had lost all my children. I would see Robbie out in the neighborhood and he acts like he don't know me. I had tried over and over again to get my shit together but I'm always falling down. Shayla had started sleeping around for drugs. It seems I'm on the outside looking at myself. My house is ran down the police already had bust up in my house. But they didn't find any drugs that time but can't be lucky everytime. My sister Donna don't even bother with me at all. The last time I had seen her she had told me I looked a mess. And she didn't have time to talk and she drove off in her brand new car. It didn't bother me at all my mom does not bother me at all either. My daddy been sick off and on so anything that he hears of his baby girl he don't listen. My family was Shayla and we got each other. Shayla was new to the game but she was learning. Well I can say one thing she was good at it. When you are a crack head and out there it is a game sometimes you lose and then sometimes you win. But there is only two places for us and that's jail or six feet under. Me and my daughter we had ran the stop, drop crack house and everything was going well. And then I didn't pay the electric for months and there goes the electric. But the party does not stop the partying continue's. All it takes to fuck up your life is the people around you to help you get there quicker. Well it was a night and everybody is chilling with the candles lit. And everybody is just sipping on wine. And Shayla bad ass have the nerve to say yell I know where Tia is at. And I lift my head up and I said Shayla repeat that. And she said again I know where Tia is at and then she went on saying that she know's where she live at. Now I'm in shock so I ask her Shayla have you talked to her and Shayla said no. But I did break into her apartment and stole her TV and VCR. Now I am hollering Shayla is you crazy why did you do that to your sister. So Shayla had stood up and said my sister she don't claim us at all. So that's why I did it and I'm going to her neighborhood and let everybody know I'm her sister. And thats why I'm going back to rob her again. Shayla holler hey mom you want to come and get some of Tia nice things. At this time Pebbles could not believe that Shayla doesn't have a heart. Not even for her own sister. Pebbles is not as strong as she want to be so she said yell I come with you the next time. Pebbles putting her head down for like three minutes. So Shayla had put everything in plan and gave instructions what to do. There is my friend who we get high with came along. But he didn't know Tia was my daughter and Shayla sister. Well everything went well but while we were in Tia's apartment. The older man were looking at pictures of Tia and he started saying that the girl looks like me and Shayla. I had grab the picture from him just a small glance, OH MY TIA WAS PRETTY. But I told him to hurry up we don't know nobody that lives in this neighborhood. I knew it was wrong to go and rob my own child. But the addiction is stronger than me. We made it out of there we had alot of stuff. I had help myself to Tia clothes oh, she had some beautiful stuff. I couldn't fit her shoes but I could fit her clothes. Well days had went by and the party was going strong we had plenty of money for our drugs. Someone had came in and announce that Shayla was arrested. My heart had drop and not only that my high. She was going to the store to buy some lighters. And the police had arrested her for breaking into Tia's apartment. I knew we were going to get caught and now the police is coming after me. Oh My God. But days went by and no police. But I did call the station and they sent Shayla to Womens Correctional Center. Finding out that Shayla had broken into other house's other than her sister apartment. So it's just me here in this bull shit that I got myself into. I am too old and I'm just tired of being sick and tired. I don't have nothing to show for anything. I don't have my children none of them. They don't even come and visit at all. I feel bad about alot of things. And I guess I will feel bad going down in my grave. Tia has going and left and started her own life without her mother and anyone else. But I did let someone rape her with my permission. And I know she will never forgive me. Well I need to stop sitting here feeling sorry for myself. And I'm going out visiting. Yes! I have some nice rags to put on. I will be looking sharp. I am over Danielle house and I was having myself a good time. Everybody was telling me how good I looked. And only thing I can do is smile. Everyone is sitting in the living room a big bang someone had knock the the door down. About four guys with guns and all I can say OH MY GOD please don't shoot me. They had shot up everyone. Only sounds you can hear is feet hitting the floor. Everything is quiet!

EPILOGUE

This is the message behind "LEFT THE GHETTO"

Being in the wrong place at the wrong time has ended Pebbles life early. She was caught up in a life. That she had all her rules to live by. Not knowing that she is hurting her children and the people around her.

The concept of this story is THE WAR ON DRUGS all around this world. We all have a Pebbles in our neighborhood. Or we have come across one of them. Our sister, daughter or cousin who is lost and think the only way out is drugs.

There is really no solution to this problem. There is more than 90,000 women are incarcerated in U.S. prisons and jails of whom 60,000 are mothers of dependent children. Sixty percent of incarcerated women in federal prisons have been convicted of drug law violations. And the dramatic increase is driven largely by mandatory drug sentences.

The fact is addiction is a disease that shatters families and costs tax payers billions of dollars. Our brothers and sisters who is caught up.

They find their self into prostitution or homeless sleeping in abandoned houses, empty apartment hallways, even abandoned cars.

Everyday our children of this world suffers. Growing up in poverty. The Ghetto, the madness, struggling to make it.

I just want to, Thank you for reading my book...And Please look out for the continuation of LEFT THE GHETTO
Title::: SHAYLA

PEACE
Ms. Kelley

0-595-31795-2

Made in the USA
Middletown, DE
14 May 2021

39637364R00054